Mary Had a Little Lamb

Characters

Narrator

Mary

Lamb

Teacher

Child 1

Child 2

Setting

Mary's house; a school

Picture Words

bag

crying

Sight Words

| be | can | good | is |
| little | look | not | she |

pet

school

Enrichment Words

back

following

soon

stay

Narrator: Most people have a cat or a dog as a pet. But Mary had a little lamb at home.

Mary: Be a good little lamb.

Lamb: Baa!

Mary: I will come back soon.

Lamb: Baa!

Narrator: Mary walked to school. At first, she did not see the lamb following her.

 Mary: Oh no! You can not come!

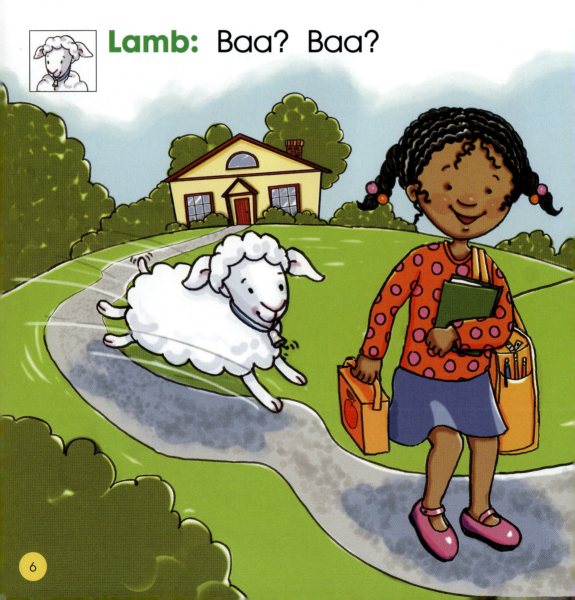 **Lamb:** Baa? Baa?

Mary: Okay, you can come. Be a good lamb.

 Narrator: Mary put the lamb in her bag. They went into the school.

Lamb: Baa! Baa!

 Mary: Shhhhh!

 Teacher: Is that a lamb, Mary?

 Mary: Yes, that is my lamb.

Child 1: Ha, ha, ha. A lamb!

 Child 2: Oh! She is so white!

 Child 1: Oh! She is so little!

 Child 2: I like the lamb!

Teacher: A lamb can not come to school.

Lamb: Baa!

Child 1: Look! The lamb is sad.

Child 2: She is crying!

 Child 1: I am sad, too.

 Narrator: All the children looked sad.

 Teacher: Do not be sad.

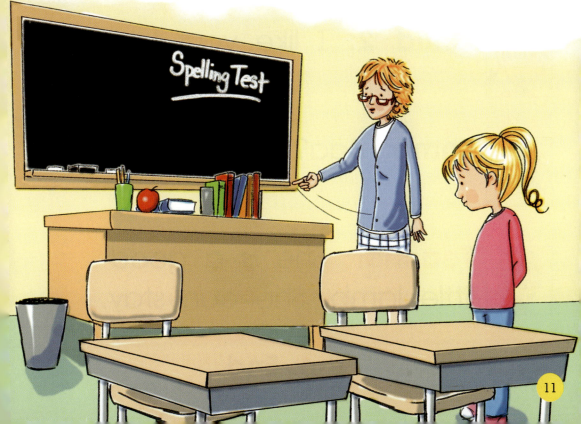

 Mary: My lamb is a bad little lamb.

 Child 1: No, she is not bad.

 Lamb: Baa! Baa!

 Child 2: I like your lamb.

 Lamb: Baa? Baa?

 Teacher: She *is* a good little lamb. She can stay.

The End